Kathleen Leverich

The New You

Greenwillow Books New York

The text of this book was set in Goudy.
Printed in the United States of America
First Edition   10   9   8   7   6   5   4   3   2   1

Library of Congress Cataloging-in-Publication Data
Leverich, Kathleen.
The new you / by Kathleen Leverich.
p.   cm.
Summary: Having lost her identity, thirteen-
year-old Abby pretends that nothing is wrong
while she searches for a new self.
ISBN 0-688-16076-X
[1. Identity—Fiction.
2. Self-acceptance—Fiction.]
I. Title.
PZ7.L5744Ne   1998
[Fic]—dc21
97-32322   CIP   AC

For Walter

CHAPTER 1

ONCE SHE REALIZED she had lost her identity, Abigail Hunter had two choices. She could admit what had happened and ask for help. She could pretend nothing was wrong and solve the problem herself.

Abby was thirteen years old and grown-up for her age. She had a horror of making mistakes. She couldn't stand to be laughed at. Being pitied was worse. If there was one phrase in the English language that would never pass Abby's lips, "I need help" was it.

"Abby's an independent girl." That's what everyone in Shorelands used to say. "Her mother died, you know, when she was just a baby."

For twelve years and eleven months Abby had been the motherless but contented owner of a fine identity in Shorelands. Then last July, just as she began to feel restless—with Shorelands, her old friends, herself, everything—*bang, bang, bang.* Abby got a new stepmother, Miranda. A new school, Urban Academy. And a new place to live: She and her dad moved to the city where he and Miranda worked.

"You'll have an exciting new life here," Miranda had promised.

Abby looked at the tall buildings, bright lights, exotic people, and believed her. Unfortunately, while she was busy looking, her identity disappeared.

How do I get a new one? wondered Abby. It was Friday afternoon, November 5, exactly nine weeks and five days since Abby had started at Urban. She stood alone in the school's crowded fourth-floor girls' room and combed her hideous hair.

"Whose hair clips are these? Can I borrow them?" called a girl at the far end of the room.

School, which Abby had liked just fine in Shorelands, was not going well here.

"Did anyone get number five right on the algebra test?" called someone.

"Thank goodness there's only one more period until the weekend!" said someone else.

Celeste Eagen, who stood right beside Abby, nudged her friend Thaïs Sarkis. "Want to spend the night at my house tonight?"

Abby sighed. Classes were bad, but these nonclass times were worse. Lunch hour. Assembly. Passing periods, like this one. All the times when kids got together to joke, talk, and relax with their friends. It was embarrassing if you had no friends. If you couldn't relax, it was a minefield. The only thing worse was the bus ride home. And, of course, the Laboratory of Ideas.

"I don't know," Thaïs was saying. "You make me get up at the crack of dawn."

"*Dawn?*" Celeste rolled her eyes. "You'd stay in bed till noon if I let you. You always oversleep."

Abby frowned at herself in the mirror.

You came to the city as somebody, said a voice in her head. You turned into no one! How could you have been so careless?

The truth was, Abby had not been careless. Abby had been deliberate. In early August, she deliberately went to the GO! department store salon and ordered her eighteen-inch braid cut off. In late August she ignored Miranda's advice and, out of all the bags in

GO!'s handbag department, *deliberately* chose the evil purse. When she started school in September and changed her name from Abby to Abigail, she did it not out of carelessness, but deliberately.

Her idea had been that "Abigail" would sound more grown-up. More . . . *metropolitan*. It did. What it didn't sound like was Abby.

And it wasn't carelessness that kept Abby off Urban's field-hockey team. And out of elected office. Abby was a stranger to Urban's teachers, coaches, and kids.

Did she have the makings of a class president? Center forward? Friend? So far, she'd been so deliberately standoffish, none of them knew.

They will know, Abby comforted herself. Just as soon as I find a new someone to be.

But where?

"Is everyone going to the party at Nina Cabot's on Saturday?" asked the girl with the borrowed hair clips.

Abby pretended not to hear. She thought of identity as a do-it-yourself project. You put yourself together. People looked at you and said, "She's okay" or "She's a creep" or "She's wonderful! Let's ask her to be our friend. . . ."

But how did you start?

Abby tried to recall how she'd become somebody in Shorelands. The more she thought, the more it seemed she had always just *been*.

"If you spend the night," Celeste was telling Thaïs, "we can do makeovers. I've got a ton of makeup my big sister threw out. Magazines, too."

"Okay, but give me back my brush," said Thaïs. She tossed her mass of curly, dark hair and reached for the hairbrush.

What would be great, thought Abby, what would be ideal, would be to find a store that sold new selves and used, right off the shelf. Like the Mercury Bookmart sold old and new books. Or the Park Drive Cycle Shop sold new and secondhand bikes.

I'd go there this afternoon, she thought. I'd pick out a spectacular one. Then on Monday I'd have it for school.

She glanced at girls lined up on either side of her at the mirror.

You have to face facts, said the voice in her head.

Abby sighed again. Her identity store was a fantasy, not real life. If she wanted to be somebody special, she'd have to invent that someone herself.

"Celeste, give me back my brush!" Thaïs grabbed

for the hairbrush in her friend's hand. She didn't get the brush, but in her friendly struggle with Celeste, she knocked Abby's comb to the floor.

Celeste picked up the comb and handed it back. "Sorry, Abigail. Thaïs is just plain clumsy."

"I am clumsy. It's true." Thaïs gave Abby a sheepish grin.

If Abby had felt sure of herself, she would have answered with a joke: "I've been meaning to talk to you about that" or "You don't know what clumsy is until you've watched me try to blow-dry my hair" or "What do you think I should do with my hair? It's been a mess ever since I had it cut."

Something to start a conversation.

She could even have said, "How's this for clumsy? I've lost my identity. Do you know where I can find a new one?"

Instead she said, "That's okay," and turned away. In the mirror she saw the two girls exchange a look. I guess she doesn't like us, said Thaïs's. Celeste's said, Too bad. At least we tried.

Abby bent to get her backpack from the floor. Her chest felt tight. Her heart pounded, the way it always did when she was scared of looking like a fool. She wondered if she had missed a big opportunity.

But what else could I do? she asked herself. It would have been dangerous to admit even to her Shorelands friends that she'd become a face and body with no one inside. To admit it to a pair of strangers—even strangers as likable as Celeste and Thaïs—was out of the question.

The three o'clock warning bell rang.

Abby headed out the rest-room door. It was hard to be alone all the time, but she was determined not to weaken. She would wait to make friends until she had transformed herself into someone all these kids would want to know.

I'll work on it over the weekend, she thought.

The weekend was just one period away.

Abby only wished that period was not the Laboratory of Ideas.

CHAPTER 2

"Settle down, people," said Mr. Mayjis. He strolled to the front of the classroom and perched on a corner of his desk.

Abby watched from her place in the last seat of the last row.

She wondered if Mr. Mayjis had ever lost his identity. She couldn't imagine that he had. Mr. Mayjis was firm and decisive. He knew exactly where he was going and what he planned to do.

Everyone in the school knew all about him. Mr. Mayjis had played professional soccer for three years before he started teaching. Now he coached both the boys' and girls' soccer teams. He did field work every summer in oceanographic studies. When the fall term began, he'd arrive back at school brimming with stories of shipboard adventures in the Indian

Ocean, on the Bay of Fundy, or off the Society Islands. Kids said that in two years, when he finished his Ph.D., he'd leave teaching to work permanently in the field.

Mr. Mayjis had his future all mapped out. He had a mission and a strategy.

People like him don't lose their identity, thought Abby with a pang of envy.

Mr. Mayjis was six-foot-five and had gray-green eyes and short curly hair. With his athletic build, crooked smile, and dark brown skin, he looked like an action-movie hero.

But that wasn't what made his science class so popular. It was what he did on Fridays.

Mr. Mayjis's Laboratory of Ideas was unlike any class Abby had ever taken. Each week they considered a "What if?" question.

Abby had known the "What if?" about the tree falling in the forest. If no one was there to hear it, would it still make a noise? But Mr. Mayjis's "What ifs" went far beyond that.

"What if in some overlooked compartment of your mind, you already know your future? What if outside our perceptions, parallel worlds spin? Is there anything to alchemy? What if ghosts exist? How would any, or all, of these phenomena affect us, day to day, birth to death?"

Mr. Mayjis graded on the originality of a student's viewpoint and on how convincingly he or she argued it. There were no right or wrong answers in this class, only arguments that were more or less persuasive.

The Laboratory of Ideas wasn't like school at all. It was like sitting at a friend's house and saying whatever popped into your head. That's why kids loved it. You didn't have to put on an act. You could be yourself.

That was why it filled Abby with dread.

"Today we'll focus on a space-time 'What if?'," said Mr. Mayjis.

Henry da Silva said, "I saw *The Time Machine* on TV last weekend. Awesome movie!"

"*That's* who you remind me of!" said Thaïs. "One of those hairy mutants who lived inside the earth."

"Morlocks," said Henry. "They were hairy, but they conquered Eloi wimps like you."

Henry and Thaïs insulted each other every Friday. Abby had thought at first they hated one another. Then she realized it was just the opposite. They were practically boy- and girlfriend.

Naturally, thought Abby. Henry was a star on the soccer field, outspoken in class, and popular with kids and teachers. Thaïs was carefree, smart, and a drama-club standout. She was also a starter on the field-hockey team.

"Space and time, people," said Mr. Mayjis. "You're all familiar with the process of osmosis. Douglas, would you define it for us?"

Douglas Cline, the science whiz and middle-school wrestling champ, laced his fingers together, turned his palms out from his chest, and straightened his elbows. His knuckles cracked. "Osmosis is the movement of fluid through a semipermeable membrane, until there is an equal concentration of fluid on both sides of the membrane."

"Excellent, Douglas." Mr. Mayjis turned to the rest of the class. "What if your life, instead of being an orderly progression of finite moments, is rather, space-and-time soup? Say that your past, present, and future exist simultaneously, separated only by a semipermeable membrane: time. Say further that stress—physical or emotional—allowed you *on certain occasions* to penetrate that membrane. Would you slip through?"

In her mind's eye, Abby saw a vast soup tureen in which all the events of her life bobbed and collided—

"Penetrate a membrane!" Henry stuck a finger down his throat and pretended to puke. "You make it sound like being a paramecium. No way would I do that."

"Okay, I'll put it another way." Mr. Mayjis grinned. "Say your past and future were places, like uptown and downtown. What if you could get to those places anytime you wanted? You'd just board a bus to last May twelfth. You'd hop a subway to November fifth, in the year twenty-something. You could even walk."

Walk back to last spring in Shorelands? thought Abby. Take a subway to ten, twelve, thirteen years from now?

She would be long gone from this school. The evil purse would be a bad memory, nothing more. Her awful haircut would have grown out.

"Would you shuttle back and forth between past, present, and future? Why or why not?"

The teacher looked from face to face. He made eye contact wherever he could. But he would have had to peer past five rows of kids to catch even a glimpse of Abby.

Abby had chosen her desk for just that reason. Mr. Mayjis could not make eye contact with her. After the first week, Abby never volunteered in class. As long as the teacher couldn't see her, she didn't have to worry about being called on. She was safe. But there was a price.

"Reactions, folks?"

Abby *wanted* to raise her hand. She wanted to enter the discussion. As unsettling as Mr. Mayjis's "What ifs?" sometimes were, they were also exciting.

In Shorelands, surrounded by lifelong friends and teachers, Abby wouldn't have hesitated. She'd have rushed in.

But not here, thought Abby. Not now.

Until she was sure she could give an answer no one would laugh at, Abby would keep her hand in her lap.

"I know! I know!" Henry's best friend, Trey Benoit, sprawled across his desk and waved his hand.

Celeste had her hand in the air, too.

Abby had spent two weeks of October classes studying Celeste. She would pick out one gesture—the way Celeste raked back her long, straight hair with her fingers, for instance—and imitate it.

She had hoped that if she got that gesture exactly right, the rest of Celeste's class president–first clarinetist–all-around everything identity would follow. Just as she had hoped that getting a haircut like the magazine model's would bring her the model's confident air. Or carrying the grown-up, hard-framed purse would bring her Miranda's. Of course, they hadn't.

At least with the finger raking, thought Abby, I stopped before the other kids noticed.

"I think the whole idea is weird," said Trey. "It's like, 'Bye, Mom and Dad. I'm going downtown to be me, five years ago.'"

Henry said, "People should live in the present. 'Be here now.' That's what Tibetan monks do, and they're enlightened."

"We'll take up Eastern religions another week," said Mr. Mayjis.

Trey said, "If we went forward or back in time, wouldn't we stay the same age, like astronauts traveling faster than the speed of light? Wouldn't we run into our older or younger selves?"

"Whoa, major warfare!" said Henry. "One self would have to destroy the other."

Thaïs rolled her eyes. "Trust a *boy* to think like that."

Abby was still thinking about going forward or backward on that bus. She imagined getting off the bus, standing on a street corner and watching her older or younger self walk by.

Celeste said, "If you met yourself, that wouldn't be warfare. *That* would be enlightening. You'd see yourself from the outside. You'd see what other people see when they look at you."

"Duh," said Henry. "Have you ever heard of a home video?"

Trey said, "On this planet, we have what we call 'the mirror.' "

Celeste was unimpressed. "A home video isn't the same. That's not what I meant. And a mirror . . ." She let her voice trail off.

"A mirror?" prompted the teacher.

Celeste raked back her hair with her fingers. She leaned forward then, as if she were sharing a secret. "I was at the GO! salon once, getting my hair cut. The walls are mirrored, and it was a Saturday so the place was really crowded. Everyone, including me, wore an identical blue smock. Okay, so out of the

corner of my eye, I noticed a girl who looked . . .
odd. I didn't know whether I liked her looks or
whether she seemed like someone I'd want for a
friend, or anything. All I knew was I *had* to get a
better look at her."

Celeste paused.

Abby thought, I got my hair cut at GO!, and it's
a disaster. Celeste got hair she can rake back with
her fingers and toss over her shoulder.

"And *so?*" said Henry.

Celeste gave him a withering look. "I leaned forward in my chair. The girl leaned forward, too. All
at once she turned from a stranger into . . . me."

"No wonder she'd looked odd!" said Trey.

"Extraterrestrial would be more like it!" said
Henry.

Celeste ignored them. "I'd been looking at a
reflection of a reflection of myself. I'd seen, just for
an instant, what other people see when they look at
me. But then it slipped away, and no matter how
hard I've tried, I've never been able to see myself
from outside again."

The classroom was silent.

"*Wooo-ooooo* . . ." Trey imitated spooky-movie
music.

Henry joined in. "W*ooo-ooooo . . .*"

"Get *out* of here!" said Celeste. But she grinned.

Abby thought, That's how you can act if you know who you are. You can say what you feel and if people make fun of it, you can laugh.

"Mr. Mayjis, I've got something!" said Henry.

"Hang on, Henry. Let's hear from someone else for a change." Mr. Mayjis scanned the room. "Abigail, let's hear from you."

Abby gazed at him in horror.

All the other kids turned to look at her.

"I forget the question," said Abby. She hoped Mr. Mayjis would call on someone else.

"Would you choose to visit your future?" he repeated. "Would you get on a bus to revisit your past?"

Abby couldn't focus on the question. All she could think of was the other kids staring at her. If she said the wrong thing . . .

"I know what *I'd* do," said Henry.

"Not now, Henry," said Mr. Mayjis. "Abigail has the floor. Abigail, you were saying?"

Abby dropped her gaze to her lap. She shrugged. "I don't know what I'd do."

For a moment no one said anything.

The teacher crossed the room to stand directly in front of her. He said gently, "Let's see if we can figure it out together. What would be a good reason to visit your past?"

Abby felt as if she were sitting in a spotlight. She knew the sooner she said something, the sooner the light would move on to someone else. She thought of the old days in Shorelands. "You could relive happy times," she said. "You could get back stuff you'd had and lost."

"And your future? The great unknown?" asked the teacher.

Abby tried to visualize. If she met her future self, and *she* had an identity—problem solved! Abby would copy it and come back to the present.

But, she thought, suppose my future self didn't have any more identity than I do now?

"I'd skip the future," said Abby. "I wouldn't go there."

"A choice we don't have in real life," said Mr. Maijis. "Class, let's explore this idea. What do you think of Abigail's decision?"

Henry stuck out his chin. "She wimped out. She's got no sense of adventure."

"Oh, so what happened to Mr. Be Here Now?" asked Celeste.

Trey nudged Henry. "What do you expect, H? Girls are less adventurous."

"Not *all* girls, Weaselhead!" said Thaïs. "Don't judge *me* by Abigail."

Abby sank low in her seat. She wished with all her might: *Let me disappear!*

Instead, the bell rang.

Abby fled.

CHAPTER 3

Everyone else rushed downstairs.

Abby headed straight for the rest room. She bent over a sink and bathed her face in cool water. She made a cup of her hand and drank.

The radiators clanked. Sleet beat against the window's opaque glass.

She straightened and pulled a paper towel from the dispenser.

The rough brown stuff felt like sandpaper against her skin. As she patted her cheeks dry, she examined herself in the mirror.

She looked as awful as she felt. Her skin was sort of greenish. Her eyes, ringed by dark circles. And that awful hair! When she had it cut, she expected to get a chin-length curtain of hair that would swing as she moved. Like the model in the picture. But the model had thick, straight, satiny hair. Abby's hair was fine, feathery, and not straight. Instead of a swaying curtain, she had gotten a used rag mop.

Abby sneezed. As she fumbled for a tissue, Celeste's mirror story came back to her. How could you *not* recognize yourself? she wondered.

She found a tissue in her backpack and blew her nose.

I would never mistake *myself* for someone else. . . .

She looked in the mirror, again. For the hundredth time she wished she had changed her name drastically on the first day of school. Not from Abby to Abigail, but from Abby to . . . Something closer to the way she felt inside. She looked at herself and thought, Arden Hunter? Natasha Hunter? *Yasmin* Hunter. If she'd done that, her life now might be completely different.

Or, she thought, everyone might have laughed.

She sneezed again as she left the rest room and started downstairs.

Abby knew she only had a few minutes if she wanted to catch the school bus, but she couldn't make herself hurry. The thought of riding home in that minibus with Celeste, Thaïs, Henry, Trey, and a dozen other kids turned her feet to stone. By the time she reached the first-floor landing, she could barely put one foot in front of the other.

At the bottom of the stairway, Abby stopped.

The lobby's marble walls and floor were alive with the sound of girls' voices. Abby recognized them. She could see the girls—a group of six or seven—gathered in the foyer beyond the French doors. The bad weather must have delayed the bus and caused them to wait there rather than head outside with the boys.

Abby did not want to join them and wait, alone, on the outskirts of their laughing, chattering group. She moved from her exposed spot at the foot of the stairs into the stairway's shadow. As she did, she banged into the water fountain she'd forgotten was there.

"Where's that bus?" said one of the girls outside the door.

Abby rubbed her bruised hip. She couldn't identify the voice.

"It is *broiling* in this foyer. I'm dying of thirst."

That was Thaïs.

"I'm going back for a drink of water. Call me if the bus comes."

Abby looked for a hiding place.

Behind her, even deeper in the stairway's shadow, stood the phone booth. She hurried to it and ducked inside.

Footsteps clattered toward her across the marble floor.

Abby started to close the door, but that made the light go on. She left the door open, pressed her body against the back of the booth, and tried to muffle her hard, rapid breathing.

Water splashed against porcelain.

Abby could see boot-clad legs, the hem of a short plaid skirt, the sleeve of an electric blue parka. This was sort of like hide-and-seek—

"Thaïs! Here's the bus," one of the girls shouted.

Splashing water ceased. Footsteps clattered fast across the floor, away from Abby. The girls' voices rose, then faded into the distance.

The lobby fell silent.

The bus would only wait in front of school for a couple of minutes.

I have to go, thought Abby.

She didn't move.

Footsteps sounded on the stairway.

Mr. Mayjis entered Abby's frame of vision. He was with someone. Abby strained to see. Mademoiselle Tych-Szabo, the Advanced French teacher.

The two teachers crossed the lobby side by side. Their murmurs were too low for Abby to make out what they said. They passed through the front doors, both laughing, and left the building.

What if? Abby asked herself. She phrased the question exactly the way Mr. Mayjis would. What if I didn't go straight home today? What if I, instead, went and found an identity store?

The oddest feeling came over her.

She sank to the phone-booth seat, pressed the door closed, and for the first time in weeks, felt hopeful. A White Pages directory and a Yellow Pages rested on the shelf below the pay phone. The cover of the White was torn. Its pages were dog-eared and soiled.

It looks as old as I am, thought Abby.

The Yellow looked brand-new.

She reached for it.

She thought as she opened it, What if I checked this directory, found a listing for Identities, and went and got one?

She found the *I*'s and paged forward. Industrial

Equipment & Supplies. She flipped backward. Hypnotherapists. Forward. She ran her finger down the page. Ice Dealers. Ice Cream & Frozen Desserts— Mfrs. & Distrs. She caught her breath.

There it was. Identities—Original & Replacement.

Below the heading, Abby found just one listing: The New You.

She ran her finger across the page to the address and phone number: 7 Nemo Place . . . 555-2329.

Abby shut her eyes in excitement. She opened them. The listing was still there.

Abby searched her backpack, fished out the evil purse, found a quarter, and pushed it through the phone's coin slot. When the dial tone sounded, she punched in the number: 555-2329.

A piercing whistle sounded through the receiver.

Abby hung up and tried the number again.

The whistle shrieked in her ear.

She sat for a second and thought. Then she tried another number. This time the call went through. A man's voice sounded from the other end of the line. "Metro Transit Authority, Route Information, Dunfey speaking."

"I want to get to Seven Nemo Place. What's the most direct bus route?" asked Abby. She told him where she was.

"You can't get from there to Nemo by bus. Six buses maybe. Your best bet is to take the subway. The station is one block away. Take the I express, downtown, three . . . no, four stops to Broadway."

Abby didn't have time to find a piece of paper. She scribbled the directions on the back of her hand.

"Change there for the eastbound double-I local. Go two stops. That's University Square. Nemo Place is right off the square."

Abby frowned at the directions. Miranda's warnings came back to her. "The city isn't Shorelands. Don't talk to strangers. Don't tell people your name or address. And above all, don't ride the subway to neighborhoods you don't know. Promise?"

Abby said, "I've never been to that neighborhood. Is it safe?"

"You want safety," said Dunfey, "ride the school bus."

The line went dead.

Abby hung up the phone. She weighed her promise to Miranda against the promise of Seven Nemo Place.

It wasn't even a contest.

Abby gathered her stuff and left the phone booth. She crossed the lobby, stuck her head out the front door, and made sure the school bus was gone.

The late afternoon was a soup of sleet, mist, and early rush-hour clamor.

A taxi zoomed by.

Abby thought, I could still get a cab and go straight home. I'd tell Dad and Miranda I felt too sick to ride the bus. That would be the sensible thing to do.

But being sensible wouldn't find her an identity.

Abby slung her backpack over her shoulder. Slip-sliding along the sleet-covered sidewalk, she found the station, squared her shoulders, and descended into the subway.

CHAPTER 4

ABBY PAID HER FARE, pushed through the turnstile, and was swept forward by the rush-hour crowd. It carried her downstairs to the platform. She had to plant her feet and brace herself to keep from tumbling over the edge and down onto the track.

The downtown I express roared out of the pitch black tunnel and into the station. Its doors opened. The crowd carried Abby aboard. All the seats in the car were taken. All the overhead metal straps were, too. Abby spotted an unoccupied two-inch space at hip level on the center-aisle pole. She grasped that.

The doors closed. The train lurched forward. Abby fell back. The train rocketed out of the station into the tunnel.

Centuries passed. The train stopped. It raced forward again. It slowed to a crawl. It stopped. It inched ahead. Sometimes the doors opened, and people got off and on. Sometimes the doors didn't. The train just sat.

Abby's forehead dripped with perspiration. She couldn't tell how many stations they had passed through. Her car was packed so tightly she couldn't see the station signs out the window. The announcements over the PA system came out as static-garbled noise. At last she overheard a nearby passenger say to a companion, "Not yet. This is only Broadway."

"Broadway?" she cried. She struggled to work her way to the exit. "Excuse me! This is my stop. Please let me by."

A man with a skull tattoo on his hand and a metal ring in his eyebrow grinned at Abby. "Darlin', we none of us can move. Better relax and enjoy the ride."

Abby's chest felt tight. Her heart pounded. Everyone in the train knew she'd made a mistake.

What a dopey girl!

She missed her stop, poor thing.

That never would happen to me. . . .

Not only that. The man talking to her had eyes the color of skimmed milk.

The doors closed. The train rocketed out of the station.

Abby thought, Why didn't I go home on the school bus? I don't know where I am. Or where I'm going to end up. What am I going to do?

In the end, the milky-eyed man helped her off at the next station. "The uptown I stops on the far side of the platform," he told her. "Take it one stop, and you'll be all set."

He waved as the train carried him out of the station.

Abby crossed the platform.

Everything happened exactly as the man had said it would. She reached Broadway and followed the signs for the double-I crosstown local. When a train pulled into the station, she climbed aboard as if she were an old hand on the subway. Casually. A little too casually. The doors closed on her. Fortunately, she wasn't sliced in half as she feared and expected. The doors' soft rubber edges squeezed, and then the doors sprang back to release her. She stumbled into the car, found a strap, and grabbed it.

Abby emerged from the station at University Square feeling relieved. And grateful that it had stopped sleeting.

The temperature must have dropped while she was in the subway. Snow fell silently out of the sky. Powdery snow, falling at a steady rate. Already an inch or so had accumulated. It covered Abby's shoes.

Abby didn't mind in spite of her chill. This snow, for whatever reason, didn't feel cold.

She glanced around again. Wrought-iron barriers closed the streets around University Square to automobile traffic. Where she stood, a park with winding footpaths and benches collected snow. Fairy lights twinkled in the trees.

Surrounding the square lay a neighborhood of quiet tree-lined streets and two- and three-story buildings. She saw a glittering laundromat-espresso bar, a renovated movie theater with an old-fashioned marquee, a fancy grocery store, a couple of expensive-looking clothing shops, a pizza place, and, in the upper stories, what looked like apartments.

Abby glanced to her right. . . .

There it was.

On the corner of the first street off the square. A street sign whose white print said NEMO PLACE.

CHAPTER 5

Abby entered the street and found number seven.

The shop windows gave away nothing. White blinds had been lowered to hide the shop's interior. A blind blocked Abby's view through the front door, too. But, above the door floated a blue neon announcement: THE NEW YOU.

Abby crunched through snow to the door. She reached for the handle. All at once, the question occurred to her. *What am I going to ask for?* She wanted an identity, yes. But what kind—original or replacement?

She let her hand drop to her side.

She'd been happy as Abby of Shorelands.

But . . . , thought Abby, I've outgrown that.

What had excited her about moving to the city,

after all, was the opportunity to shed her old identity. To assume a new one. That was the identity she had come downtown to get.

But will I be able to explain what I want? she worried. Would a salesperson understand?

Snow accumulated in her awful hair.

Abby put the worries from her mind. Anyone in the business of selling original and replacement identities must have developed a sense of what a buyer was looking for.

You want safety, ride the school bus.

The only way to find out was to go inside.

Abby grasped the door handle and pushed.

The door was locked.

She saw a button and pressed it.

A buzzer sounded.

Abby grasped the handle. The door swung inward. Abby stepped through.

She stood blinking for a second against the bright lights. Her eyes adjusted, and she took in her surroundings. Mirrored walls. Varnished wooden floors. Counters lining the side walls. Sinks lining the rear . . .

Abby's heart sank.

The New You was a hair salon.

And not a very successful one, Abby realized as she looked more closely.

No stylists combed and clipped at the stations. No clients sat in the chairs. There were no chairs. In the middle of the salon space there were, instead, two couches and a coffee table. Off to one side stood a music stand.

Two women sat on the couches. A third sat on the receptionist's counter just ahead of Abby. They looked older than college age but younger than thirty-year-old Miranda. All three stared at her.

"Who are you?" asked the woman sitting cross-legged on the counter. Her ash-blond hair was cut very short and wispy. A pale crescent-shaped scar shone on her left cheekbone. She was dressed in a silver leotard and tights, athletic shoes, and a short, drapey, rose-colored wrap skirt. On her lap a gray cat purred. She leaned backward straight-armed on the counter. "Whoever you are, you've come to the wrong place."

"I thought she was Daas, Gail. That's why I told you to buzz her in," said the woman on the right-hand couch. She was small, thin, and dressed in close-fitting, faded jeans. Her beige V-neck sweater was oversized, as if she'd borrowed it from a boyfriend. She had pale blue, slightly protruding eyes, a complexion the color of extra-light toast, and a mass of crinkly black hair that had been pulled back from her heart-shaped face and secured with tortoiseshell combs. She frowned at Abby. "I thought you were my boyfriend. What address are you looking for?"

Abby couldn't say, I was looking for an identity. Instead she lied. "I was shopping. I noticed your sign and thought this was a hair salon."

"I told you we should disconnect that sign," said the crinkly-haired woman.

The third woman, curled up on the other couch, shook her head. "No way!" Her blond hair was swept up in a French twist. She wore a moss green business suit that matched her eyes. A pair of brown high-heel pumps lay on the floor beside the couch where she had kicked them off. "Every night when I turn the corner and see that sign, I get excited.

THE NEW YOU

It's like an invitation: 'Cross this threshold and be transformed.' "

"I've crossed it a million times. No one's transformed me," said the crinkly-haired one. "I wouldn't hold my breath if I were you."

The business-suited one folded her arms and raised her chin. "The sign stays."

Abby felt more disappointed than she could bear.

"This isn't a salon," said the woman on the counter—Gail, the crinkly-haired one had called her. "There's a good one around the corner on Euclid. Try there."

Abby turned to go. Her head seemed to be floating above her body. Her legs felt weak and rubbery. The salon door looked a million miles away.

"Hey, she's going to faint," cried one.

"Catch her!" said another.

Abby felt three pairs of hands grasp her.

"Can you make it to the couch?" The three women helped her to a seat.

"Get her a glass of water," ordered Gail.

"Are you sick?" asked the business-suited one.

Abby sank into the couch. She felt uncomfortable around strangers. She always had. But, she realized as these women fussed over her, she didn't feel uncomfortable now. She felt oddly at ease. "I forgot to eat lunch," she said. That wasn't strictly true. She hadn't forgotten lunch; she'd been too anxious about the Laboratory of Ideas to eat. "And even though it's cold outside, I got hot coming down here on the subway."

"So you're from uptown?" asked the crinkly-haired one. She handed Abby a glass of water.

The business-suited one said, "Are you going to be okay? What's your name?"

Abby took the glass and swallowed. Miranda had told her, "Never give your name to strangers." She took another sip and said, "My name is Yasmin."

"Yasmin." Gail had resumed her seat on the counter. She stroked the gray cat and sighed. "I wanted to be called Yasmin when I was your age. I would have sold my little sister to be called Yasmin. Actually, I would have given Olivia away for nothing."

The crinkly-haired woman regarded Abby through narrowed eyes. "I don't believe Yasmin *is* your name. But if that's who you want to be, I'll be . . ."—she tapped her lower lip with an index finger—"I'll be Artemis."

The business-suited woman clapped. "I'm Lorna! I've always wanted to be Lorna."

She reminded Abby of an excited little kid.

Lorna turned to Gail. "Who are you going to be?"

"I already heard you call her Gail." Abby put down the glass on the coffee table.

"And that's who I'm going to stay," said Gail. "Are you feeling any better?"

Abby wasn't, but the women had been so kind, it didn't seem polite to say so. She nodded.

Artemis threw herself back on the couch. "Won't your parents wonder where you are, Yasmin? Do you usually wander around the city alone?"

Abby had forgotten all about getting home. "What time is it?"

Lorna glanced at her wristwatch. "Quarter past five."

Artemis bolted upright. "Don't let me forget, I have a nine-thirty audition tomorrow. I can't oversleep. It's for a part that could change my life."

Abby didn't want to move. She was tired and, at the same time, utterly relaxed. Still, she had to think about getting home.

She struggled to her feet and approached the counter where Gail sat. "Can I use your phone to call my parents?"

Gail glanced at her friends.

"She seems harmless," said Lorna.

Artemis cocked her head. "We can't very well throw her out in the snow."

The gray cat hopped from Gail's lap to the counter-top. It paced the counter's edge, back and forth, back and forth. . . .

Abby stood and watched the cat. She forgot the women. She forgot her parents and the phone. She forgot everything except the cat's steady back and forth, back and forth. . . .

The gray cat stopped. It locked gazes with Abby. It dropped to a crouch—

"Look out!" said Lorna.

It was too late.

The gray cat sprang.

CHAPTER 6

T HE CAT STRUCK Abby full in the chest.

The impact bowled her backward. She grasped the cat and held it to her. Its head rested underneath her chin. It worked its way deep into the crook of her chest and throat. It purred.

"Look at that! Omen *likes* Yasmin," cried Lorna.

Artemis threw herself back on the couch again. "I see it, but I don't believe it. Omen hates everyone except Gail. Nasty cat. She spits at me."

The cat settled deeper into Abby's embrace. Abby's whole chest vibrated with its purring.

"Omen isn't nasty. She's skittish," said Gail. She turned to Abby and frowned. "Do you have catnip in your pocket or something?"

Abby shook her head.

Lorna said, "I remember the day you got her. I'll

say she was skittish! I can't believe that was thirteen years ago."

"If *Omen* thinks Yasmin is family, I say it's definitely okay to let her use the phone," said Artemis. She slid sideways on the couch. "Sit, Yasmin. That cat is pretty hefty to wear as a brooch."

Abby sat, all the while holding the cat. "His name is Omen?"

"*Her* name," said Gail.

Omen jumped from Abby's chest, to the couch, to the floor.

"Look at you. Your forehead's all damp." Artemis reached out and pushed Abby's too-short bangs from her brow. "Take off your jacket and give it to me."

Abby shrugged off her backpack and parka.

Artemis hung Abby's things on a wall peg alongside coats, jackets, hats, umbrellas, a handbag or two, backpacks, a field hockey stick, and a musical instrument case, long and narrow, hard and black.

Gail had reached back to retrieve a cordless phone from underneath the counter. She handed it to Abby. "Here you go. Just keep your call local."

The three women watched as Abby punched her number into the phone.

A piercing whistle sounded through the receiver. "Ouch!" said Artemis.

Abby tried the number again.

The whistle shrieked.

"The snow must be causing a problem." Abby handed the phone back to Gail. "The same thing happened earlier this afternoon when I tried to make a call."

"Will your parents be worried?" asked Lorna.

Abby hesitated. "They don't get home from work until six or six-thirty," she said. That much was true. "If they call our housekeeper before that, they'll figure I stopped at a friend's. I do that a lot. Then I start having such a good time, I forget to phone." She couldn't tell a lie much bigger than that one. But the women seemed to accept it. The idea that she could have friends didn't seem to shock them.

She looked from one to another. She hoped she wouldn't sound rude, but she had to ask. "Why do you live in a hair salon?"

Artemis exchanged a look with Lorna.

Lorna shrugged. "You might as well tell her the truth."

Artemis turned to Abby. She sighed. "We are the ghosts of hairstylists past, doomed to haunt abandoned salons until all the terrible haircuts we gave in life grow out."

Lorna tipped her chin to stick her nose in the air. "We are selfish princesses, forced by a powerful enchantment to assume the lowly chores and identities of the minions we once scorned."

Abby didn't mind that they were making fun of her. She grinned. "No, really. Why?"

Gail said, "We live here for three reasons: It's cheap. It's cheap. It's cheap."

"There's office space upstairs." Artemis pointed to the spiral stairway near the sinks. "We turned it into bedrooms. There's a kitchen out back, and one and a half baths."

"Legally, we shouldn't be here," said Lorna. "But when the hair salon went out of business, the landlord couldn't find a tenant, so he rented to us, under the table, without a lease. He can kick us out anytime he finds a hair stylist who wants to take over the spot."

"Meantime," said Artemis, "we get a duplex apartment in the neighborhood of our choice for next to nothing. Gail has family connections. She convinced the landlord."

"Gail convinced *us*," said Lorna. "I work in public policy at the mayor's office. If anyone found out about this arrangement, it would be good-bye to my job."

Abby looked at Gail. From the moment she had stepped into the salon, Gail had been the one her eyes gravitated to. Abby couldn't tell why. Lorna was prettier and more friendly. Artemis was the one who seemed daring and wild. Gail stroked Omen, listened to the others, and said little.

Lorna went on, "I was going to say absolutely no to the apartment. But then Gail told us her secret."

Artemis cupped her hands around her mouth and stage-whispered, "What Gail wanted was to live near a certain university professor."

"You promised not to tell anyone!" said Gail.

Artemis rolled her eyes. "Who's Yasmin going to tell?"

"I would never tell anybody," said Abby. Her interest perked up. For the first time since she'd entered the salon, Gail seemed flustered.

Lorna leaned closer to Abby. "As you can see, Gail is nuts about this guy. He teaches just around the corner, at the university. At least he does when he's not away on an oceanographic expedition."

Gail yanked a book from beneath the counter. A textbook. *Small Animal Anatomy*. She slammed it down on the countertop. "I never should have told you. I knew it. It's a mistake *ever* to admit *anything* to anyone."

Artemis nudged Abby. "We're her best friends, and she never tells us what she's up to. When she wants something, instead of telling people or asking for help, Gail pretends she couldn't care less."

Gail stuffed the textbook in a backpack. "I may have been like that once. I'm not that way anymore."

Artemis grinned. "You're better than you used to be. At least you trusted us this once with a secret. And just think, if you hadn't, we wouldn't have moved in here. You wouldn't be thrown into the path of the man of your dreams three, four, five times a week."

Lorna turned to Abby, "Gail's vet school classes are way across town. Her only hope of running into him was to live here."

"Admit it," said Artemis. "It pays to share problems with other people."

"Maybe. Maybe not. We'll see," said Gail.

Without thinking, Abby volunteered, "I have a teacher who's an oceanographer."

"No kidding?" Gail's eyebrows shot up. "Maybe they know each other. What's your teacher's name?"

Abby was sorry she'd opened her mouth. The likelihood was that Mr. Mayjis *did* know Gail's professor. He might even know Gail. The two of them were about the same age. He would tell Gail that "Yasmin" was really Abigail, the most pathetic misfit in the school.

"My teacher is only a student oceanographer," she said. "Not like your professor. He probably wouldn't want me to say."

"You're as bad as Gail," said Artemis.

Lorna grinned. "Everything is a secret."

Gail frowned at Abby. She turned abruptly and marched upstairs.

Abby's forehead felt damp again. She combed back her hair with her fingers.

"My, my, Yasmin." Artemis shook her head pityingly as she surveyed Abby's hair. "I can see why you were looking for a salon. That haircut is not doing you any favors, girlfriend."

"My haircut is fine!" said Abby. Her chest felt tight. Her heart pounded. She could just hear

Artemis thinking, How pathetic. Doesn't she have any taste? I'd rather die than walk around looking like that.

"I didn't mean to insult you." Artemis looked startled. "I just think a good stylist—"

"Quiet, Artemis," said Lorna. She studied Abby's head. "Artemis may lack tact, but she's right. Your hair's too fine for that kind of blunt cut. The shape doesn't do a thing for your face."

Heart pounding, chest tight, Abby opened her mouth to defend the haircut—

She stopped.

Why should I? she asked herself. The haircut *was* a terrible mistake. Why put on an act? Why pretend it wasn't?

Abby felt the tightness in her chest ease. Her heart stopped pounding. It was as if a heavy weight had lifted from her. She felt like . . . herself. "The stylist warned me of all those things," she admitted. "But I'd seen a picture in a magazine. The model was so beautiful that I told him I wanted the cut anyway. Now I have to wait for it to grow out. It's taking forever."

Artemis reached out a hand. She pushed Abby's

hair this way and that. "Why wait?" she asked. "Why not cut your hair shorter? That's what I'd do."

Lorna narrowed her eyes to gaze at Abby. "It's true. I've been thinking ever since you arrived that you ought to have a cut like Gail's."

Gail came downstairs dressed in jeans and carrying a fat loose-leaf binder. Abby studied her haircut. It was what magazines called a "waif."

"Gail's natural color is the same chestnut as yours," said Artemis. "Highlighting gives it those blond flecks. You could get highlights, too. Only a few because you're a kid. . . ." She let her voice trail off.

Abby saw her expression change from excited to puzzled.

Artemis raised a hand to her forehead. She gave her head a hard shake and then turned to stare at Lorna and Abby. "I just experienced déjà vu big time!"

"I felt it, too!" gasped Lorna. "It was exactly as if I'd lived that moment before."

Abby was still busy thinking about her hair. "I've never imagined cutting it really short."

"We could do it right now," said Artemis. "I'm an expert haircutter, and Lorna here used to highlight everyone's hair in our college dorm."

"We'll give you a total makeover!" said Lorna.

As Gail walked past the couches, she gave Lorna a bat on the head. "Leave the poor kid alone! It's late. She should go home."

Home? Abby didn't want to go home.

"I want a makeover," she said.

"Come on, Gail," coaxed Lorna. "Let us do it. We'll give her a whole new identity."

"Her friends won't even recognize her," promised Artemis.

Abby could see Gail was on the point of saying no. She didn't understand why it should be up to Gail, but she knew it was. She also knew, without understanding how she knew, that she, Abby Hunter, had it in her power to make Gail say yes.

"What if we conducted the makeover like a scientific experiment?" Abby suggested. "We could take notes on everything Lorna and Artemis do, and then track how it changes my life."

"What if?" Gail gave her a searching look. The scar on her cheek shone whiter.

She's dropping her objections, thought Abby. Again, she didn't know how she knew. She just knew. She was certain.

Lorna and Artemis knew, too.

"Get a chair. I'll get the highlighting kit," shouted Lorna as she ran up the stairs.

"Get my scissors while you're up there," shouted Artemis. She ran to the kitchen for a chair.

Abby stole a look at Gail. She glanced in the mirror then and wondered, How will I look as her?

CHAPTER 7

Ninety minutes later, Abby sat on a kitchen chair at one of the hairdressing stations. She still couldn't answer that question. All the while her hair was being highlighted, washed, conditioned, cut, and blown dry, Abby had avoided looking at her reflection. She was afraid to look now.

"Ta-dah!" Artemis stood to the right of Abby's chair at the counter. She shut off the hair dryer, stood back, and examined her creation. "I should give up acting and become a professional makeover artist. Look at you!"

On Abby's left, Lorna said, "I wish we had before and after pictures, Yasmin. You're a totally different person."

Gail stood behind Abby's chair. She studied Abby's reflection in the mirror. "If you'd told me a haircut could make such a difference, I wouldn't have believed you."

"The highlighting is what does it," said Lorna. "Yasmin, how do you like the results?"

Abby couldn't speak.

It wasn't because she was stunned by the apparition in the mirror. Although when she examined the girl with short, tousled, ash-blond hair and a mysteriously appealing face, stunned she was.

Abby couldn't speak because while Lorna was highlighting and Artemis was cutting, Abby's throat had gotten so sore, it hurt even to swallow. Her joints ached. So did her head. The temperature in the salon seemed to go from frigid to overheated and back to frigid in a scissor's snip.

I'm definitely coming down with something, she thought.

But who cared when she'd been so miraculously transformed? "I love it," she croaked.

"You sound terrible!" Artemis turned from the mirror to look at her. "You *look* terrible. I mean, you look terrific, but sick."

Lorna put a hand to Abby's forehead. "You're burning up. How do you feel?"

"Awful," Abby admitted. "Can I lie down somewhere?"

"We've got to get you home," said Gail. "If we call you a cab, do you think you can make it to your house okay?"

"We can't send her out alone," said Lorna.

Abby made a pillow of her arms on the counter and rested her head.

Gail glanced at her watch. "It's seven-fifteen. I've got class in fifteen minutes. I can't cut it."

"I have a date with the senator's aide. Finally," said Lorna. "What about you, Artemis?"

Artemis sat on the counter beside the discarded scissors and hair dryer. "Daas should be here any minute. He promised to run lines with me for tomorrow."

"Call the cab. I don't need help. I'll be fine," croaked Abby. She didn't want to become a problem.

Gail hesitated.

"Really." Abby's head hurt when she spoke.

"Okay," said Gail, "but you have to promise: Have someone phone us the minute you get home. Here's our number." She scribbled it on a scrap of paper and handed it to Abby.

Abby recognized the number she had tried from school: 555-2329.

Gail picked up the phone, punched in a number, and waited. "Town Taxi? We need a cab right now at Seven Nemo Place."

"Leave us your number, Yasmin. We'll call tomorrow and check on you," said Lorna.

Abby took the pen and paper Lorna offered. She wrote her phone number and put it on the counter.

Lorna helped her on with her parka.

"How many minutes?" Gail was still on the phone. "Thanks. Oh, and make sure the driver honks *and* waits. Some drivers don't even come to a full stop. They just speed away. Okay. Thanks."

She hung up and turned to Abby. "It'll be about five minutes. Do you think you can last that long?"

Abby didn't. "I'll be fine," she lied.

Artemis got Abby's backpack from its peg. "Promise you'll come visit. Remember the experiment. You have to let us know how the makeover changes your life."

A purse hanging from the same peg as her backpack caught Abby's eye. It was the twin of her evil purse. Except this one was worn with use. "Whose purse is that?" she asked.

"That purse?" said Artemis. "That purse belongs to Gail. Once upon a time, she wanted to be a sophisticated uptown *lady* like her mother."

"Stepmother," said Gail. "We all make mistakes."

Lorna ran a finger over the purse's scarred leather. "I give Gail credit. She carried it when none of us would have been caught dead with a bag like that. She made it . . . not fashionable, but at least acceptable." She turned to Gail. "You were courageous."

"She was stubborn." said Artemis. "She still is."

A horn tooted.

"There's the cab!" said Gail. She ran to the door and leaned out. "She's coming!" she called. "Wait!"

Abby followed unsteadily.

Gail turned to her. "Are you sure you're all right? Do you want me to ride with you?"

The pale scar shone on her cheekbone.

"I'll be okay," said Abby. Her joints ached. Her arms and legs felt like cooked spaghetti. All she wanted was to crawl into her bed and pull the covers over her head.

The taxi horn tooted impatiently.

Abby felt Gail's hands on her shoulders. Gail guided her out the salon door and across the sidewalk. Snow blew in her face. Gail seated her in the cab and spoke to the driver. "This girl is ill. Get her home as fast as you can. Here's something extra for your trouble."

Abby saw her hand the driver a fistful of dollar bills.

Gail turned back to her. "Remember," she said. "Phone us." She straightened and swung the door shut.

Abby wasn't sorry to be on her way home. She'd had the most thrilling afternoon of her life at The New You. Once she felt better, she'd go back to thank the women properly for all they'd done. She might even tell them the truth about who she was and how she'd ended up at their door. But for now, all she could think about was lying down in her own bed.

"Where are we going, young lady?" the driver asked through a grille in the security barrier.

"Nine-oh-nine Park Drive," croaked Abby.

The cab driver slid shut the grille.

Abby felt the cab pull away from the curb.

Gail watched from the sidewalk. She hugged herself and waved through the snow. "Bye, Yasmin!"

Abby liked her. A lot. Even if she was touchy.

She thought, Before I leave, I should tell her who I really am.

She fumbled with the window's crank handle.

It stuck.

She tried again. "Come on!"

No matter how hard she tugged, the handle refused to turn.

The cab sped up.

The driver made a hard right to enter the uptown expressway.

Abby gave up on the window. She sank back into the cab's lumpy seat.

I'll tell her when I phone, she thought. I'll say, Guess what? I have this dopey secret. . . .

CHAPTER 8

THE CAB PULLED UP at the awning-covered entrance to Abby's building.

Snow was falling heavily now. Abby stepped from the cab and could barely see the potted trees beside the building door. Snow hit her in the face. It was over her ankles. As she fought her way to the front door, it filled her shoes.

The doorman, Rafael, was nowhere to be seen.

Abby staggered across the lobby to the elevator. It took all her concentration, but she managed to locate and hit the UP button.

Machinery whirred. A thump sounded. The elevator doors slid back to let her in. A moment later Abby found herself gliding upward toward the twelfth floor.

As floor after floor passed, Abby realized she

couldn't remember getting from the sidewalk into the lobby. She couldn't remember entering the elevator. She thought groggily, One minute I was in the cab, now I'm here. . . .

The elevator bounced slightly under her feet.

The elevator doors parted. Abby stumbled into her family's front foyer. She grasped the edge of the library table for support. "Dad?" she called. "Miranda? Mrs. Sharma?"

No sound came out of her mouth.

Abby couldn't understand it. Her throat was sore, yes. It was hard to speak, and it hurt, but she could do better than that.

She mustered her strength and tried again.

"Dad? Miranda? Mrs. Sharma?" Her voice was a peep.

But—Abby glanced around—there didn't seem to be anyone home, anyway. Lamps were lit, as usual, but no one came to meet her. The apartment was silent.

Everyone's probably out looking for me, thought Abby.

She shrugged off her backpack. She shrugged off her parka.

They fell to the floor, and she left them.

She stumbled through the living room. She caught sight of herself in the big gilt mirror.

It was the same ash-blond, tousle-haired waif she'd encountered half an hour ago, downtown.

I look wonderful, Abby thought in disbelief.

But she still felt weak and ill.

She continued the arduous journey over carpets and down corridors to arrive at her own room. Once there, she yanked back the bedspread and crawled under the covers. School clothes, wet shoes, and all.

The next thing Abby knew, she was lying in her pajamas in bed. Sunlight streamed in at the windows.

Abby felt weak. She was thirsty. She tried to sit up but was so overcome by dizziness she had to lie down again. Her head stopped spinning, and she was aware of feeling . . . happy.

At first she couldn't imagine why. Then Abby remembered.

My new identity.

Peace settled like a comforter over her. Abby shut her eyes. She drifted back to sleep.

Sometime later she became aware of people in the room.

"Her fever's down. She's on the mend." Abby heard her dad whisper.

"After all those days! What a relief," whispered Miranda.

Abby opened her eyes. "What day *is* it?"

Her father sat on the foot of her bed. "It's Tuesday, November ninth. Eight-oh-five A.M."

Miranda smiled down at her. "You've been sick with flu, sweetheart. But you'll be up and about in a day or two."

Before they could scold her for disappearing on Friday, Abby rushed to apologize. "I knew you'd worry when I was late, but I stayed at The New You anyway. I'm sorry. I was having such a good time."

Miranda looked puzzled. "Sweetheart, you weren't late. You didn't disappear. You felt sick, and instead of riding the bus home from school, you wisely took a cab."

Abby shook her head. "I *thought* of doing that, but instead I took the subway downtown. I knew I wasn't supposed to . . ." She shrugged. "But I did."

"Honey, Rafael met you at the door," said her father. "Mrs. Sharma brought you up in the elevator and put you to bed. When she phoned our offices, it must have been four-forty-five, five o'clock at the latest."

"No," said Abby. She couldn't understand how her parents could be so dense. "I didn't get home until quarter to eight. You weren't here. Neither was Rafael or Mrs. Sharma."

Miranda gently brushed Abby's bangs from her brow. "You were sick. Your mind played a trick on you. You had a very vivid dream."

Mrs. Sharma entered the room carrying a tray. She backed up Abby's parents. "Rafael helped you from the cab. I helped you upstairs and put you to bed. You were one sick girl." She rested the bed tray over Abby's lap. "Eat that soup now. Drink lots of water."

"I can prove it," said Abby. She gave her head a shake and raised a hand to finger-comb her short, highlight-filled hair. "How do you explain my haircut?"

Her hair felt dirty and matted. It also felt strangely long. It felt . . . shoulder-length.

"A mirror," cried Abby. "Give me one. Please!"

It was inconceivable. But it was true.

Abby's hair was the same shoulder-length, chestnut mess it had been before she discovered The New You.

CHAPTER 9

ABBY DIDN'T WANT to talk. She didn't want to eat. When Miranda looked in on her later that afternoon, Abby turned away.

Miranda sat on the edge of the bed. She said, "I have an idea. What if we ask Roger to cut your hair exactly the way it was in your dream?" She pulled Abby's hair back from her face and studied her. "That *is* becoming. I don't know where you came up with it—in a dream or at The New You—but it's the perfect style for you."

Miranda was trying to cheer her up. Abby knew that. She also knew the problem was not her hair. The problem was, she still had no identity. She'd lost her three grown-up friends. There would be no visits to The New You. Getting a haircut wouldn't change any of that.

Still, when Miranda picked up the phone to make the salon appointment, Abby didn't protest.

"Two o'clock, with Roger, on Saturday," said Miranda. She hung up and went to check her computer for E-mail from work.

Tuesday afternoon faded into evening. Abby's already depressed spirits sank with the sun. Still, a part of her refused to accept what seemed obvious. That part insisted, "It was no dream!"

At five-forty-five, Abby asked for the Yellow Pages.

Her father brought it to her. After he left the room, she opened to *I* and began turning pages. Identification—Security Systems was followed by Image Consultants. Identities—Original & Replacement, did not exist.

Abby phoned directory assistance. They had no listing for The New You. Or not, at any rate, for a downtown hair salon. There was a New You listed, but it was a cosmetics boutique at GO!

Abby searched her memory for the phone number she had tried from school. The number eluded her.

At six-fifteen, she called the MTA. "I'd like the best subway route from the Urban Academy to Nemo Place."

The route information woman told her to take the downtown I express to Broadway and board the Riverside bus.

"Why not the double-I local to University Square?" asked Abby.

"The double-I has been out of service for three years," said the woman. "If you want to ride that line, you'll have to wait another three at least while we replace track. And there is no such stop as University Square. There is no University Square in the city that I'm aware of."

When Miranda brought her dinner on a tray, Abby asked for the street atlas.

"It's at my office," said Miranda. She was a broker for a commercial real-estate firm. "I'll take a break for lunch tomorrow and bring it home."

Wednesday at noontime, Abby sat in bed with the *Metropolitan Street Directory and Gazetteer* open on her lap. According to the directory, the MTA woman was right. University Square did not exist. Plus there was no street named Nemo. Or there was, but only a four-block lane in the rundown former Mirror District.

"Most of the buildings in that section are abandoned factories and glazier's workshops," said

Miranda. She traced the district's outline with a finger. "Mirror manufacturing was an important industry sixty or seventy years ago."

"The neighborhood I went to wasn't rundown," said Abby.

"It's true the whole area is ripe for renewal. In seven to ten years, there'll be gentrification. The university, which is now a good half mile away, could buy up properties for expansion. But for the moment"—Miranda looked up from the map and shook her head—"it's just plain dismal."

Abby stared at the useless map. "University Square had espresso bars, fancy grocery stores, and clothing shops. It was like where we shop in Park Village, except the people were younger."

"Ah-ha!" Miranda touched a finger to the tip of Abby's nose. "The plot thickens. University Square bears an uncanny resemblance to Park Village. Your friends' hair salon/apartment shares a name with a cosmetics counter at GO!"

"I'd never seen that counter," said Abby. She knew where Miranda was leading. She was determined not to follow her.

"Don't you see, Abby?" Miranda looped a stray

wisp of hair behind Abby's ear. "You ran a high fever for two days and nights. You slept and dreamed for two days after that. You mixed up what you've seen awake, on the street, with what you saw in your dreams."

"No," said Abby.

"Yes," said Miranda.

Abby fell back onto her pillows. "If I could just remember their phone number, I'd call them. Then you'd have to believe me."

Miranda kissed Abby's forehead. She stood and started for the door. "Take your pills. Ask Mrs. Sharma for anything you need. I'll see you this evening."

"Miranda?" Abby called after her. "Can I get a cat?"

"A cat?" Miranda paused in the doorway. She looked down at her belly and gave it a pat. "You'll have a baby sister in less than five months. Won't that be enough?"

Abby didn't want to hurt her stepmother's feelings, but the answer was no. "The baby will belong to everyone. A cat would be just mine."

Miranda seemed to consider for a minute. She

nodded. "It's a fine idea. You get better, and we'll find you a cat. Maybe next month."

Abby wanted the cat today. Right now. But Miranda had already left.

Late that afternoon, Abby remembered.

Have someone phone us the minute you get home. Here's our number.

She hurried to the front closet and got her parka. She searched every interior pocket and compartment. She turned the parka inside out—

A scrap of white paper fluttered to the foyer floor.

Abby's heart skipped a beat.

She scooped up the paper. She turned it over.

It read, "Inspected by Number 356."

That night Abby awakened to see snow falling past her windows. Her bedside clock said 12:13 A.M.

Abby slid out of bed. She crossed the room. The carpet felt scratchy under her bare feet. She knelt on her window seat and pressed her palms to the cold windowpane. She rested her forehead against it, too. She gazed out.

Traffic flowed in a slow but steady stream down Park Drive.

Snow muffled the street noises and created a halo around every light. A million lights. A billion. Maybe more.

Abby gazed across the snow-covered park. She gazed downtown in the direction of Seven Nemo Place. She concentrated with all her might. I *know* you're out there, she thought.

But Abby didn't know. Even as she thought it, she didn't really believe.

She concentrated again. Lorna, she thought, Artemis, Gail, give me a sign.

Snow continued to fall. The city lights glimmered. Traffic flowed steadily down Park Drive. No sign came, and Abby, at last, gave up. Her parents were right. There was not now—there never had been— a Lorna, Artemis, or Gail. The only way back to The New You was via the rapid transit system inside Abby's own head.

Abby turned from the window. She trudged across the carpet and crawled back into bed.

CHAPTER 10

FRIDAY MORNING DAWNED cold and clear.

Abby unwillingly got ready to go back to school. She pulled her hair back, twisted it up, and fastened it with a clip. She examined herself in the mirror. It didn't look like the makeover cut, but it looked better than before. She slung her backpack over her shoulder. She pulled from deep inside her closet the hard-framed leather purse.

Abby turned it over in her hands.

It didn't look evil. It didn't feel cursed or treacherous. She recalled now why she had chosen it last summer from all the other bags at GO! Because it was different. Unlike any bag she had ever owned. She had expected to open it and find, inside, a brand-new life.

She unsnapped the metal clasp. The fragrance of

new leather spilled out. But now there was something else.

Who are you? You've come to the wrong address.

We can't throw her out in the snow!

Come back and visit us. Promise you will.

Abby shut the purse. She knew she'd be asking for trouble, but . . .

I won't keep it in my backpack anymore, she decided. I'll carry it, no matter how much kids laugh.

She slid the purse over her arm.

"Abby, let's go!" her father called from the corridor.

Abby examined herself one final time in the mirror.

"Ab-*by*!"

She hurried to join her father at the elevator.

Thanks to a lucky break, her dad had an early, uptown appointment. He was taking a cab and said he'd drop her off. For this one morning, Abby wouldn't have to face the kids on the bus.

Rafael held the door as she slid into the cab. "Good morning, Miss Hunter. You certainly look healthier this morning than you did after school last Friday."

How would you know? Abby wanted to ask. Instead

she said, "Thank you." She turned her attention to praying for bumper-to-bumper traffic and major delays.

Jefferson Avenue was unaccountably empty. The cab zoomed north. Every red light it approached flashed green. In mere minutes, the taxi screeched to a stop in front of Abby's school.

Her dad waited for her to get out.

The driver waited.

Abby didn't want to. She stared at the gray stone fortress that was Urban Academy and wanted to go straight home to bed. She knew she couldn't, but . . .

All at once the oddest sensation came over her. Abby had the feeling she was being watched. She craned her neck and looked from one towering building to another.

Go, girlfriend!

You can do it, Yasmin!

Abby took a deep breath, kissed her dad, and got out of the cab.

She felt the three women's eyes on her as she climbed the school's front steps.

Look, Gail, she's carrying a purse like yours!

The girl has nerve. Way to go, Yasmin!

Abby held her head higher. She tugged the massive front door open.

Show those kids who has an identity!

She stepped inside.

One class, one passing period, one instant inside the building was all it took for Abby to lose her cheering squad and come face-to-face with reality. Abby couldn't mix. She couldn't make friends. She still had no identity.

Take 11 A.M. sports class.

Abby was a better-than-average basketball player. Much better than average. When the two team captains chose up sides, Abby stood a little apart. She tried to look as if she didn't care whether she was picked or not. Just in case. It was a good thing she had. Because, sure enough, she wasn't picked. Not until the very end.

Take 1:15 algebra class.

Ms. Hunsicker handed back the previous Friday's test. She announced that Abigail Hunter had scored the one and only perfect 10. Abby looked at her paper and acted like it was no big deal. Douglas Cline had scored the only 9.5. Douglas raised clasped hands over his head like the heavyweight champion of the world. After class, kids rushed to slap Douglas on the shoulder. "How do you do it?" they asked. No one said a word to Abby.

And now, at five past three, her least favorite class was about to begin. Abby thought of faking a relapse and getting a pass to the nurse's office. Instead she slid into the last row, last seat, of Mr. Mayjis's classroom. She chewed her lip and waited to begin another session of the Laboratory of Ideas.

The bell rang.

Mr. Mayjis closed the classroom door and crossed the room to perch on the corner of his desk. He peered past the five intervening rows of seats until he found Abby. "You've had quite an ordeal, Abigail. How are you holding up today?"

Everyone turned to look at her.

Abby felt her face redden. "Fine, thank you," she said. Don't call on me, she thought, and I'll be even better.

Mr. Mayjis apparently didn't read minds. He kept right on talking to her. "I understand from Dr. Wilcox that your fever took you on a rip-roaring dream journey."

Abby froze. Who had told the school director? Her dad? Miranda? They both probably had. She became aware of Henry and Trey staring at her. Of Celeste and Thaïs watching her as they whispered, back and forth, behind their hands. Abby studied her desktop and said, "I guess it did."

"A mysterious phenomenon, dreams," said Mr. Mayjis. He stepped forward to pluck a Masters of the Universe comic from Neil Mustaph's lap and toss it onto his own desk. "You may retrieve it after class, Mr. Mustaph. For now, let's all turn our attention to dreams. Do they show us the world as it truly is? Foretell the future? Explain the past? Or are they simply—and much less romantically—a product of cranial nerve cells' random firing? No one knows. Maybe one of you folks will make the scientific break-through that explains dreams, once and for all. Mean-while, Abigail, would you be willing to share your dream with us?"

Abby stared at the teacher. Her chest felt tight. Her heart pounded. What are you *doing* to me? she thought. Are you *trying* to make me look like a jerk?

"You don't have to. I ask because I myself have never had a dream so vivid that hours, even days after I woke up, I felt it to be true. I envy your experience," said the teacher. "I'd like to know more about it. I suspect your classmates would, too."

The classroom fell silent.

Abby heard a siren wail four stories below, in the street. She heard a plane roar, thousands of feet overhead. She wished she were anywhere, *anywhere* but this classroom. She wished—

Tell them, Yasmin! Tell them we were no dream. We're counting on you.

You can't expect her to risk that! Not in a classroom where she has no friends. What if everyone laughs?

How's the girl going to get friends if she doesn't let people in on her problems? How's she going to get a good haircut if she won't admit the one she has stinks?

"Abigail?" said Mr. Mayjis.

Abby remembered how she felt when she had stopped defending her haircut. If she could feel that way again now . . .

"I'll tell what happened," said Abby. The tightness in her chest eased. Her heart stopped pounding. She did not feel light and unburdened. But maybe later she would. "I guess it was a dream, but it seemed— It still seems real to me."

"We're all ears," said Mr. Mayjis.

Abby chose her words carefully. "For a long time I've been hunting for . . . something I've lost. Last Friday after school, I happened to be in the phone booth . . . the one downstairs in the lobby."

She stole a glance at Thaïs. Thaïs gave no sign of guessing that Abby had been hiding from her. Abby went on. "I noticed the Yellow Pages. Just as a joke, I decided to look up this thing I'd lost in the directory. Sure enough, there it was."

Abby told about the call that wouldn't go through. About the MTA and Dunfey. "So I took the subway—one express and one local—way downtown. When I missed my stop on the express, a man with a skull tattoo and milk-colored eyes helped me. I got to the store, but it had gone out of business. The space had turned into . . ."

Abby stopped. She glanced at the other kids.

Why did she stop? This is where we come in. Tell about us, Yasmin!

Abby didn't feel like telling about Artemis and the others. Some things she preferred not to share. "The space had turned into something else. Still, I went inside. Then, even though I didn't expect to,

I *found* what I was looking for. That's when I started to feel sick. I took a taxi home and went to bed. Four days later I woke up. I looked for the thing I'd found. It was gone. I checked our Yellow Pages. The listing was gone. Even the local subway line was gone. Closed, since three years ago, for track replacement."

"Wow!" said Henry.

Abby shrugged. "My parents say it was a dream. I can't prove it wasn't."

"But you're not convinced?" suggested Mr. Mayjis.

Abby shook her head. "In a dream, impossible things happen. There are big gaps in space and time. When you try to tell someone about a dream, it doesn't make sense. One person turns into another. One second you're in an airport, the next, in your old kindergarten classroom. This wasn't like that. Everything made sense as it was happening. Everything makes sense to me now."

"Well, folks," Mr. Mayjis stood. "What do you think of Abigail's adventure?"

"Cool!" said Henry.

"It's so mysterious!" said Celeste. "It's sad, too, but in an exciting way."

Thaïs turned to Abby. "What was the thing?"

Abby knew what Thaïs meant, but she pretended not to.

"The *thing!* What were you looking for?" demanded Thaïs.

Abby said, "It's private. I don't want to say."

"Come on, tell," coaxed Thaïs. "Please? I'd tell you."

Abby doubted that.

"Thaïs, I think you heard a no," said Mr. Mayjis. "Abigail was generous enough to share her dream. Let's respect her privacy."

"I know!" shouted Trey. "The Yellow Pages! In the lobby phone booth. That'll have the listing. There's your proof." He sat back and grinned at Abby. A friendly grin. For the first time.

Abby was so surprised, she didn't answer at first.

"Excellent idea, T-man!" said Henry.

Abby nodded then. "I thought so, too. But the directory I used Friday was brand-new. The one in the booth today is beat up and ancient. I checked first thing this morning. There is no listing."

Abby felt sad just remembering.

"Bum-mer." Henry shook his head in sympathy.

Abby felt sad, but, she realized, not *as* sad.

Nowhere *near* as sad. More than sad, she felt buoyant. As if an enormous burden had vanished. She felt for the first time in months like . . . herself.

In fact, when Mr. Mayjis caught her eye and nodded his approval, Abby couldn't help but grin.

CHAPTER 11

For Abby, the rest of the period passed in a haze. She was too distracted to pay attention. She had an identity. She was Abigail, the girl who'd had the strange but cool experience.

What did it mean? How had those odd events happened? The other kids argued about it until the final bell rang.

When it did, Mr. Mayjis raised a hand in farewell. "Have strange but cool weekends, all of you."

Abby gathered her books. She thought of stopping to speak to him. She wanted to say "Thank you for helping me. You're the best teacher I've ever had. I like you so much. . . ."

Of course she couldn't. But she had to let Mr. Mayjis know she was grateful—

"Hey, Abigail?"

Abby looked up.

Celeste and Thaïs stood in front of her desk.

"That dream? Was it *really* as convincing as you said?" asked Thaïs.

It sounded to Abby as if she didn't believe one word. "I told exactly what happened. If you think I'm lying—"

"Don't be so touchy! All I did was ask." Thaïs raised her hands. "I believe you, okay?"

"You must have been so upset when you woke up," said Celeste.

Abby shrugged. "I was upset. I still am. I'd give anything to find a way back into it."

"Right," said Thaïs, "and find that *thing* you were looking for. What was it?"

"Abigail doesn't want to say. How many times does she have to tell you?" asked Celeste.

Thaïs ran a finger over Abby's purse. "Hey, you're carrying your 'tea with the queen' bag again. Do kids really use them where you come from?"

Abby shook her head.

"I knew it!" said Thaïs.

"You told us they did!" said Celeste.

Abby shrugged.

"Do you honestly like it? What made you pick it?" demanded Thaïs.

82

Abby looked at that bag on her arm. "It was different. That's why I chose it. I thought if I carried it, I'd be different, too."

"Were you ever right!" said Thaïs.

Celeste rolled her eyes. "Earth to Tha-ï-ïs . . . Abigail doesn't mean different from us. She means different from herself. A grown-up instead of a kid." She turned to Abby. "We want to help search for that place you went."

"Can we?" asked Thaïs. "We're great detectives."

Abby hesitated. She wanted Celeste and Thaïs to be her friends. But she wasn't sure she wanted them to poke around looking for Artemis, Lorna, Gail, and The New You. At least not now. Maybe when she knew them better.

"We'll be free all day tomorrow," said Thaïs.

"Not *all* day," Celeste corrected. "I've got a clarinet lesson at nine in the morning."

Thaïs grabbed Abby's arm. "You could come to my house or Celeste's, and we could plan our investigation."

"Tomorrow?" Abby felt relieved to have an excuse. "I can't. I'm getting my hair cut at GO!"

Celeste looked disappointed.

"What time?" asked Thaïs.

Abby slung her backpack over her shoulder. "Not until two, but—"

"Perfect! We'll go with you," said Thaïs. "First we'll stop in the cosmetics department and see what free samples they're giving away, then we'll eat lunch and then go for your haircut. Celeste and I will supervise."

Abby hesitated. "My stepmother was going to come—"

"Your *stepmother!*" said Thaïs. "Does she think you're in nursery school? Tell her to find some other way to spend her Saturday. Your friends will look after you."

Abby felt the way she had in class. The moment when Trey grinned at her. "I guess I could."

"It's settled. Meet us at my apartment at eleven. We can walk from there to the store."

Abby was suddenly aware of Mr. Mayjis straightening papers at his desk. He hummed. He didn't seem at all conscious of their presence.

"We'd better go if we're going to catch the bus," said Thaïs.

As she and Celeste hustled Abby out the classroom

door, Abby glanced back. Mr. Mayjis appeared as oblivious to their departure as he had been to their presence. Until he looked up, caught Abby's eye, and winked.

CHAPTER 12

Sun shone on Saturday morning. The November air felt crisp. Abby walked down Washington Avenue. Celeste was on her right; Thaïs, on her left.

This is exactly the way I imagined everything, thought Abby in amazement. This is what I wished for, every day, for weeks and weeks.

Still Abby couldn't shake a certain sadness.

She missed Artemis, Lorna, and Gail.

You only spent one afternoon with them, said a voice in her head. They were figments of your imagination, not real.

It didn't matter to Abby. She missed them.

I'll never know whether Artemis got the part she was trying out for, she thought. Whether Lorna will get to keep her job and keep going out with the senator's aide. Whether Gail will tell the oceano-grapher how she feels about him.

Abby sighed.

She thought, And they'll never know the truth about me—

Celeste's clarinet case hit her knee.

"Sorry, Abigail," said Celeste. She shifted the case from her left hand to her right. "I should have dropped this at home after my lesson."

The bump to her knee didn't hurt Abby. But it jarred loose a memory. Something about . . . not her knee, not a similar autumn day . . . something about a hard, black instrument case, just like Celeste's—

"Aren't you glad you're getting your hair cut?" asked Thaïs.

Abby nodded. "I'm getting the same style as a friend of mine. I'll show you." She opened her purse. She took out a picture of a model with Gail's haircut.

"A waif," said Celeste.

Thaïs studied the picture. She glanced up at Abby. "You should get highlights, too. On chestnut hair like yours, it would give it those blond flecks."

The oddest feeling came over Abby. It felt like falling in a dream and snapping awake. As if she'd lived this moment before. She slipped the picture back in her bag. "I am getting highlights. Just a few. Until I'm older, my stepmom said."

"Great!" said Thaïs.

"Did you notice the cat in the picture?" asked Celeste as they walked. "It was Persian. I love Persian cats."

"I'm getting a cat, too," said Abby. "Not like that one. Just an ordinary cat."

Celeste wheeled on her. "I *love* cats. My mother and brother are allergic, so we can't have one. When are you getting yours?"

Abby shrugged. "I wanted to get one right away. Miranda said as soon as she has time to look into it. Maybe next month."

Thaïs grabbed Abby's arm. "I just remembered! The tropical drinks place on Fourth Avenue? O Mango? They have a whole litter of kittens they're giving away. Not exactly kittens. They're a couple of months old. Let's get you one right now."

"Tha-*i*-ïs," Celeste frowned. "Abigail just told you, her stepmother said next month."

"My stepmother always says next month. That doesn't stop me," said Thaïs. She turned to Abby. "You'll be saving her trouble. She won't have to 'look into it.' "

Abby thought she'd better speak to Miranda first.

Thaïs dragged her forward. "Come on, Abigail! It's destiny."

"Tha-ï-ïs—" Celeste glared.

Thaïs ignored Celeste. She led Abby a couple of steps away. "Listen, Abigail, we have to do something about your name. It's okay, but it doesn't really sound like you. You're more a—"

"Vanessa," said Celeste. "That's what I thought the first time I saw you. I thought you looked . . . not exactly stuck-up, but as if you were used to more interesting kids than us."

"You did?" Abby was stunned.

They walked by a woman selling hot dogs from an umbrella-covered pushcart.

Celeste nodded. "You acted more grown-up than us. You did stuff no one else would have dared."

"Like carrying that purse," said Thaïs.

A bus pulled up at the stop just ahead. Its doors sprang open. No one got off. Five people climbed aboard.

"You had a past we didn't know anything about. We thought you were mysterious," said Celeste.

Abby shook her head in confusion. "You were wrong."

Celeste shrugged. "That's the way you looked to us."

Vanessa? Abby couldn't get over it.

They passed a subway entrance. People rushed headlong down the stairs. Other people climbed blinking into the daylight. Both groups had to step over a crowd of pigeons gathered at the top of the stairs. The birds were squabbling over the remains of someone's dropped hot dog.

Abby realized she was scanning the faces of passersby. Women. Young women. That crinkly-haired one, was that Artemis? No. That tall blond, could she be Lorna? No. There was Gail! Right behind the guy peddling watches and sunglasses— No, it was not.

She forced herself to concentrate on her flesh-and-blood companions. "I'm not mysterious. I'm not stuck-up. I just didn't think anyone would like me."

"We both did," said Thaïs. "But you were so standoffish. And you got so angry when I kidded you about that purse. We were afraid to talk to you after that."

Celeste nodded. "It's true, but I still thought you should be Vanessa."

Abby turned to peer at a threesome of women—

No.

You can hope, wish, and look all you want, said the voice in her head. They are not going to appear.

"We can't call her Vanessa," Thaïs was saying. "It's got to be something to do with her real name. Otherwise the boys will make fun. Especially Henry and Trey."

Celeste said, "Henry isn't such a fabulous name. He should change *his* before people make fun of him."

"How about *Duh? Silva?*" Thaïs laughed at her own joke.

Celeste nudged Abby. "What did the kids in your old school call you? What does your family call you? Abby?"

Abby nodded.

"That's no better," said Thaïs. She threw out her arms to stop Abby and Celeste. "Come on, we have to cross. There's O Mango."

Abby hadn't been to the drink stand since summer. Then, she and Miranda used to stop at the take-out window most afternoons.

The take-out window was shuttered now, for winter. The shop windows were fogged with steam. Abby followed Thaïs and Celeste toward the door of the tiny storefront, sandwiched between Ragnol's Variety and Dunfey's Hardware.

Abby stopped short. She stared up at the hardware sign.

"What's wrong?" asked Celeste.

"Nothing," said Abby.

A big brown dog appeared at the hardware store door. He barked furiously through the glass but wagged his tail, too.

Dunfey is a pretty common name, thought Abby. She turned to the others. "Let's go see those kittens."

Ten minutes later, Abby was following Thaïs out the door. Against her chest she held an eight-week-old gray female kitten. Its claws gripped her parka and made soft popping noises as they penetrated the fabric and pulled back.

"She matches your eyes," said Thaïs.

Celeste stroked the kitten's head with one finger. "Cats live a long time. You'll have her for ten, maybe even twenty years."

Twenty years? thought Abby. I'd be thirty-three—

"Look out!" said Thaïs.

Inside the hardware store, the dog's lips curled back from his teeth.

"He sees the kitten," said Celeste.

The dog lunged at the door, barking furiously.

The cat scrambled up Abby's shoulder to escape.

"It's okay." Abby gripped her harder.

The dog threw himself at the door. He barked and rattled the glass. The kitten struggled frantically. She twisted in Abby's grasp.

"Calm down," said Abby. "Ow!" she cried.

The kitten's claws pierced her cheek.

CHAPTER 13

"IT WASN'T HER FAULT," said Abby. "That dog scared her, and I was in the way."

Abby sat on the marble wall of a raised bed of shrubs and ornamental trees that bloomed in front of a forty-story office building. The building had a drugstore at its base.

The kitten rested calmly against Abby's chest. Celeste dabbed her cheek with an alcohol swab from the drugstore.

"It's not so bad. One claw went deep, but the rest is just scratches," said Celeste. She turned and threw the swab in a trash basket.

Abby stood. Her legs felt a little rubbery but all right.

The three girls started down the block toward GO!

"Lucky she missed your eye," said Thaïs. She

reached out a finger to scratch the kitten under the chin.

The kitten spit.

Thaïs jumped back. "Nice temperament. What are you going to call her, Lethal Weapon?"

Abby rested her healthy cheek against the cat's soft fur. "I'm calling her Omen."

"Omen . . ." Celeste tried out the name.

Abby lifted Omen to reposition her. "Some friends of mine have a cat named Omen. She's thirteen. I won't be seeing them anymore, so I don't mind copying."

"What friends?" asked Thaïs. She walked backward facing Abby.

"Just friends," said Abby.

They had reached GO!'s revolving doors.

Celeste stopped them. "What are we going to do with Omen? Pets aren't allowed inside the store."

Abby looked at the doors. She looked at Omen. "I'll put her inside my parka. She'll be safe, and no one will know."

"Not unless she mews," said Thaïs.

"We'll mew, too," said Celeste. "We'll cover for her."

Abby gently slipped Omen into her jacket.

"I'll help." Celeste unzipped the parka halfway. She cinched the waist cord tight.

"All set," said Abby, and led the way through the door.

It was only eleven-fifteen, but the store was crowded.

"Cosmetics department first," said Thaïs.

"Wait!" Celeste let a model with a perfume atomizer spritz her.

Abby tried to recall. Had Artemis, Lorna, or Gail used perfume?

The model turned to Abby.

"No, thank you," said Abby. She followed her friends into the maze of cosmetics counters.

Thaïs let a consultant smooth moisturizer into her cheeks.

"We offer an excellent lemon-balm astringent, too," said the consultant.

Thaïs collected samples for all of them. She handed one pair to Abby and one to Celeste.

"Look!" Celeste pointed.

A signboard in the aisle said: COMPUTERIZED MAKEOVERS 11 A.M.–2 P.M. AT NEW YOU COSMETICS.

"I've heard of those!" said Thaïs. "My cousin got

one at a store in Chicago. They point a video cam at you. Your face appears on a giant monitor. You tell them what you want to change, and they do it by computer to the image. You can change your nose, your eyes, your chin—"

"Are they free?" asked Celeste.

"It says Complimentary." Abby pointed to the last word on the sign.

"Let's go," said Thaïs. She headed deeper into the labyrinth of counters. "I'm going to change everything."

Abby and Celeste hurried after her.

They reached the New You counter. There was already a line.

"I *hate* lines. I hate waiting," said Thaïs. She crossed her arms to sulk.

"It's only four people," said Celeste. "It won't be long. You can go first." She turned to Abby. "What changes are you going to ask for, Abigail?"

"Abigail . . . Abby . . . I don't like either one," said Thaïs. "Can't we think of a better name? Omigod!"

"What?" asked Celeste.

Abby hugged the bundle inside her parka. She glanced around, expecting another big dog.

"It happened!" said Thaïs. "I didn't get what you were talking about. But it just happened to me."

"*What?*" demanded Celeste.

"What?" echoed Abby.

"My reflection! In that mirror." Thaïs pointed. "I saw it and didn't realize it was me."

Abby frowned. She felt skeptical, but one look at Thaïs's expression convinced her. This wasn't theatrics. It wasn't a stunt. Thaïs blinked rapidly. Her mouth gaped. She was telling the truth. Still, Abby was puzzled. Just as she'd been when Celeste told about her experience, in class. How could you *not* know yourself?

"What did you see?" asked Abby.

"Myself from the outside. The person other people see," said Thaïs. "That was so weird! *Why* didn't I get a better look? I am *such* an idiot."

By the time Thaïs managed to calm down, she was sitting in the makeover seat, before the video cam.

"I need a little personal information first," said the New You consultant. "That way we can keep your preferences on file. Name, address, age."

Thaïs gave the information. The consultant keyed

it into the computer. "Now, Thaïs, for your makeover today . . . ?"

"I'd like my nose less bumpy, my chin less pointed, and my eyes deeper set and wider apart. Don't touch my skin color. I like it toasty. Oh, and fuller cheeks. I'm going to be an actress when I grow up. I need to look more generic, less ethnic."

Abby listened in astonishment. How did Thaïs know so specifically what she wanted? How had she managed to analyze her features in such a professional way?

The New You consultant keyed commands into the computer. The face on the video screen, Thaïs's face, began to change.

Abby began to feel sad. Sadder than she could bear. This makeover reminded her of her downtown makeover, just eight days—just a lifetime, ago. But, that had been an authentic metamorphosis. This was a magician's party trick.

"You're all done, Thaïs," said the consultant.

Abby wasn't sure, for the better. The girl on the screen was pretty. But she wasn't unusual. Quirky. She wasn't Thaïs.

"I can show you how to make each of these selfenchancing alterations, cosmetically, with New You products," the consultant was saying. "Your makeover record will include your computer-enhanced image, plus a list of the items you'll need to re-create this look."

The printer spit out Thaïs's record.

"I'll think about the products," said Thaïs as she took the printout from the consultant.

The consultant signalled Celeste to take the makeover seat.

"You won't mind if I don't buy anything?" asked Celeste.

"I don't work on commission," said the consultant.

Abby guessed she was Vietnamese or Cambodian. She wore a white silk blouse. Her woolen skirt was ankle length, pleated, and black. A red leather belt encircled her tiny waist. A matching red-leather watchband encircled her left wrist. Her chin-length hair hung straight and smooth. When she moved, it moved, a black silk curtain.

Like the curtain of hair I used to want, thought Abby. She saw now that it would have looked all wrong on her.

"Besides, the company views this sort of session

as an investment," the consultant was saying. "You may not buy anything today, Celeste, but if you have a pleasant experience, you may come back. And then—" She turned to Thaïs and Abby and raised an eyebrow. "Who knows?"

Celeste's face appeared on the video screen.

"And you would like to look . . . ?"

"Less like a cheerleader," said Celeste. "I'm going to be an international lawyer or a public-policy analyst, so I have to develop a more intellectual and exotic look."

Abby was as startled at Celeste's request as she had been by Thaïs's. Why would Celeste want to change anything? Celeste was perfect.

The consultant didn't bat an eye. She nodded as if she understood perfectly what Celeste meant and went to work on the keyboard.

Celeste's eyes changed from down-turned crescents to almond-shaped. Her small, straight nose length-ened, narrowed, and acquired a bump. Her cheeks collapsed inward. Her cheekbones changed from smooth to angular. Her lips collapsed slightly while her mouth grew wider. . . .

Abby thought, She's still beautiful. But she isn't

Celeste. As a matter of fact, now she looks more like Thaïs.

Celeste's makeover record rolled out of the printer. Celeste took it and stood.

The consultant signalled Abby into the makeover seat.

CHAPTER 14

ABBY SAW HER FACE materialize, huge and uncertain, on the video screen. She felt Omen, inside her parka, clawing her way up her chest.

Abby had no idea what changes to request.

She was satisfied with herself, for now. The only thing she wanted was to have her "dream" proved true. She wanted Artemis, Lorna, and Gail actually to exist. She couldn't very well ask for that. The consultant was a makeover expert, not a miracle worker.

Omen poked her head out of the parka collar under Abby's chin.

"I see what profession you're going to follow," said the consultant. "You're going to be a veterinarian."

Abby tried to excuse herself. "This kitten? I just got her. Otherwise, I'd never have brought her into the store—"

"Don't fuss, honey. I won't turn you in," said the consultant. She leaned closer to Abby and frowned. "That's a nasty cut, young lady. I have a niece your age, and if she had a cut as deep as that one, you can be sure we'd have our doctor look at it."

"Is it that bad?" asked Abby. She glanced up at her image on the video screen. The scratch *was* deep. She started to rise from the seat. "Maybe I should skip the makeover and go put something on it."

"No way, Abigail!" Thaïs pushed her down by the shoulders. "We'll take care of you after you finish here. A couple of minutes won't make a difference. What features do you want changed?"

Abby struggled to come up with something. "I'm getting my hair cut this afternoon. I'd like to see how that will look."

"Bor-ring!" said Thaïs.

"She's getting a waif cut," said Celeste. "Let's see that."

The consultant nodded. "We can do that. What else?"

Abby couldn't think of a thing. She finally said, "I'd like to look grown-up. Really grown-up." It was the best she could do.

"I've got it!" said Thaïs. "Don't change Abigail's

features. Age her. Make her exactly the way she'll look when she's, say—"

"Twenty-six," said Celeste.

The consultant, her hands poised above the computer keyboard, turned to Abby. "Is that what you want? A waif haircut and age twenty-six?"

Abby chewed her lower lip. She had an uneasy feeling about this. "You can't do that, can you? Show how I'll look years from now?"

"Who knows what this computer is capable of?" said the consultant. "Let's give it a test. Let's see if it can show you as you were—say, five years ago."

"I had a braid then," said Abby. "Just one. And longer bangs."

The consultant nodded. She punched in commands. "Minus five years. Plus some baby fat."

"There you are!" said Thaïs.

"Is that the way you looked?" asked the consultant.

A larger-than-life eight-year-old gazed at Abby from the screen. Her eyes widened as they met Abby's. Her jaw dropped, and she raised a finger to her lower lip.

Abby couldn't take her eyes off the child. Finger still at her lip, Abby nodded. "That's me."

"You were cute," said Celeste.

"On to the future," said the consultant.

"Oh, boy!" said Thaïs.

Abby knew she should say no. But a part of her thought, Let's see, just for a second. . . . She cradled Omen more firmly inside her jacket. "I'm ready," she said.

The consultant typed furiously. Nothing happened. She frowned. She typed in two more commands.

The image on the monitor dissolved. Symbols flashed.

The consultant leaned back in her chair and stretched. "Might as well relax, Gail. This may take a few seconds."

Thaïs gave the consultant a "hel-lo-o" look. "Gail?"

"That's her name, isn't it?" said the consultant.

Celeste shook her head. "Her name is Abigail."

The consultant shrugged. "My niece is Abigail. We call her Abby. Abigail. Gail. It's all the same."

Abby felt lightheaded, but in a different way from when she'd had the flu. It was as if her mind had turned to soup. She couldn't make sense—

"Honey, I am not joking about that scratch of yours." The consultant tapped the back of Abby's hand with a polished fingernail. "You need stitches. Without them, you're going to have a scar. Right there, on your cheekbone."

The soup of Abby's mind turned transparent.

She raised a finger to touch her cheek. . . .

"Look!" Celeste pointed to the monitor. "There you are."

Abby didn't need to look. She knew who she'd see.

. . . *I knew* she was no Yasmin!

I *didn't know. I didn't recognize her at all. Did you, Gail?*

She looked . . . interesting . . . to me. But I didn't understand why.

Space and time, folks. What if the past, present, and future exist simultaneously?

"Earth to Abigail," said Thaïs.

"I thought we were going to call her Gail," said Celeste.

The consultant gave Abby's hand a gentle shake. "Oh, Miss Hunter? Here is your printout. Wake up."

Abby blinked.

Two aisles away an elevator bell rang. A dozen clashing fragrance samples thickened the air.

Omen shifted position on Abby's chest.

"You were practically in a trance," said Celeste.

"See anything interesting?" asked Thaïs.

Abby-Abigail-Gail looked at her friends.

"You did see something, didn't you?" said Thaïs.

Abby stood. She took her printout from the consultant. "Yes," she said. "I did."

"Well?" Thaïs demanded.

Celeste leaned closer. "What was it?"

Abby stuffed the printout in a pocket. What had happened was too big. It was so . . . confusing.

I'm not ready to tell people, thought Abby. Not anyone. Not even them. Not yet.

"I'll tell you all about it," she promised. "Someday."

"Someday?" Celeste looked disappointed.

"Why not right now?" asked Thaïs. She raised clasped hands to her chin. She made her eyes big and pleading like a little kid. "Please tell. We'll be your *best* friends."

Abby looked at the two girls. A feeling more complicated than happiness crept over her.

"I know," she said. "You will."